MW00903837

Star of the Show

Della Ross Ferreri
Pictures by Tony Weinstock

For ★★★★★
Be the star of
your own show!

Della R Ferreri
January 2010

Shenanigan Books
www.shenaniganbooks.com

Text copyright © 2009 by Della Ross Ferreri

Illustrations copyright © 2009 by Tony Weinstock

All rights reserved.

No part of this book may be reproduced or utilized in any form or by any means, electronic or mechanical, including photocopying, recording, or by any information storage or retrieval system, without permission in writing from the Publisher.

Inquiries should be addressed to Shenanigan Books, 84 River Road., Summit, New Jersey, 07901.

ISBN: 978-1-934860-03-8

Printed in China

The illustrations were created with acrylic paint on watercolor paper.

Library of Congress Cataloging-in-Publication Data

Ferreri, Della Ross.
 Star of the show / written by Della Ross Ferreri; illustrations by Tony Weinstock.
     p. cm.
 Summary: When Francine and her brother Max play pirates or put on a circus, she always gets the best parts until Max declares that he, too, wants to be the star of the show.
 ISBN 978-1-934860-03-8
[1. Brothers and sisters--Fiction. 2. Play--Fiction.] I. Weinstock, Tony, ill. II. Title.
 PZ7.F372St 2009
 [E]--dc22

2009003224

To my fabulous nieces and nephews:
Jamie, Kelly, Katie, Kyla, Kiley, Zach,
Ben, Marina, Nick, Grace and Violet,
and of course, my own stars,
Catherine, Emily and Matthew.

Special thanks to my writer friends,
for bringing out the best in my stories.
You deserve the spotlight, too!
– Della

Thank you to my parents and sister
for your love and support,
without which this endeavor
would not have been possible.
– Tony

When Francine and her little brother, Max, play pirates, Francine is the captain of the ship…and Max has to walk the plank.

When they play explorers, Francine is the
leader of the expedition…and Max carries all
the supplies.

When they play animal hospital, Francine
is the veterinarian...and Max is the sick dog.

That's how Francine and Max always played…

until one day Max came up with his own idea.

"Hey, Francine," said Max. "Let's put on a circus."

"Okay," she said. "I'm the star of the show. You can be my assistant."

"You always get the best part," said Max. "This time I want to be in the show."

But Francine was already grabbing things from the toy box and tossing them to Max.

"Hold the flashlight. Line up the animals in the audience. Then I'll be ready to start."

"Let me do a juggling act," said Max.

"You're the assistant, and I'm the star, remember?" said Francine. "You hold the spotlight and cheer for me."

Max picked up a ball, tossed it high in the air and caught it behind his back.

"See! I can be a star, too!"

"Not bad, Max. But the balls are for me!"

Francine turned to the audience. "Ladies and Gentlemen, Boys and Girls, Presenting the **Fabulous Francine! Star of the Show! Let the circus begin!**"

Francine started juggling. She tossed a ball high in the air and *almost* caught it behind her back. Quickly she kicked it away. "Ta da!"

Max just stood there.

"You're not cheering," said Francine.

"You missed the ball," said Max. "And I'm bored. I want to be in the show!"

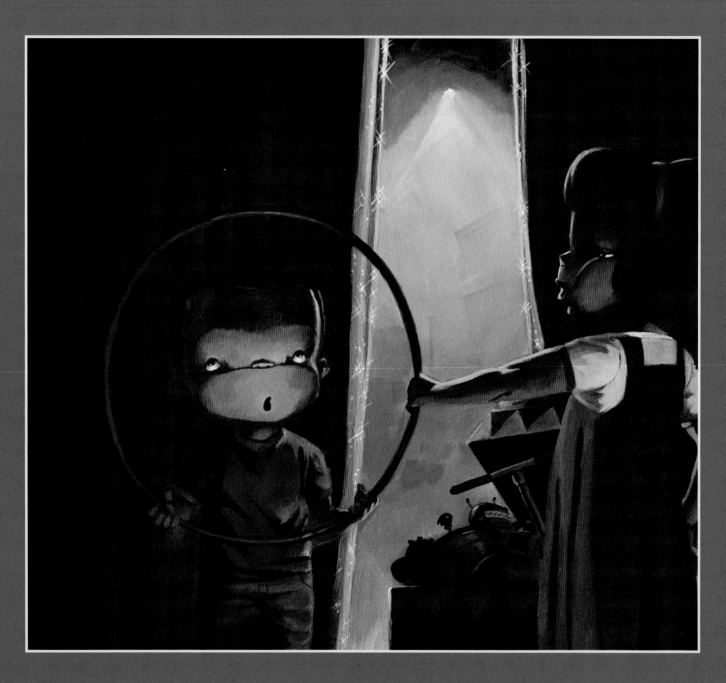

"Oh, all right," said Francine. "Here, hold the tiger hoop."

Max took the hula-hoop and bowed.

"I've asked my assistant to help," said Francine, "for this dangerous act."

"Very dangerous," said Max.

"Have no fear," said Francine. "The tigers have been trained by the greatest master in the world."

"Who, me?" said Max.

"Not you!" said Francine. "I'm the greatest master in the world!"

One by one the tigers jumped through the hoop and circled the ring. "Ta da!"

She raised her eyebrows and stared at Max. "Cheer for me!"

"Oh, I forgot," said Max. He put down the hoop and clapped. "Shouldn't you cheer for me now?"

"All you did was hold the hoop," said Francine. "Anyone can do that."

"Ladies and Gentlemen, Boys and Girls," announced Francine.

"Now for my grand finale - The Fabulous Francine on the wild, white stallion!"

"Your grand finale?" said Max. "Wait, Francine! No fair! I didn't get a chance yet!"

He grabbed his pogo stick.

"It's my turn now," he said, bounce bounce bouncing around the room.

"Stop that! I'm the star of the show!" yelled Francine, rocking so hard on her rocking horse that it shimmied across the floor.

"I can be a star, too! Watch this!" shouted Max.

But Francine was rocking too hard… Max was bouncing too fast…

The door flew open. "What's going on?" asked Mom.

"It's a circus," said Francine. "Want to watch?"

"Hmmm," said Mom, looking around. "You might need a little more practice."

"Yeah, we do," said Max.

"Can you come back for the two o'clock show?" asked Francine.

Mom smiled. "Save me a front row seat."

"We need a plan," said Francine. "Let's make a list of the circus acts. I'll go first."

"I want to go first," said Max.

"I'm older," said Francine.

"The circus was my idea!" said Max.

"I'm the Fabulous Francine," said Francine. "You're just the assistant."

"I don't want to be just the assistant," said Max. "And if I don't go first…I quit!"

"Quit?" said Francine.

"Yeah, you'll have to play by yourself," said Max, and he stomped out of the room.

By myself? thought Francine. *How am I supposed to put on a circus by myself?*

She tried to get the tigers to jump through the hoop, but the hoop kept falling over and the tigers toppled to the floor.

She tried propping up the flashlight while she juggled, but the light rolled off the shelf and hit her in the head. "Ouch!" she cried and she chased after Max. "Wait, Max! Wait for me!"

"What if you go first, then I do the juggling act? And…can you help me catch the ball behind my back?"

Max grinned. "Fine. I'll go first, and I'll help you juggle…but remember, I'm not your assistant…and we both do the grand finale."

At two o'clock, Francine and Max were ready.

"Ladies and Gentlemen, Boys and Girls...and Mom," announced Francine, "Presenting the **Fabulous Francine**... and the **Magnificent Max!**

Let the circus begin!"

Max was perfect on the pogo stick.

Francine was a juggling genius.

Together they were a hit with the hula-hoops.

"Now for the Grand Finale!" announced Francine.

Francine amazed the audience with her super stunts on the wild, white stallion.

"Ta da!" she called.

Max wowed the crowd with his magnificent scooter maneuvers.

"Ta da!" he shouted.

"Bravo! Bravo!" said Mom.

"That was the best circus!" said Max.

"And we were both stars of the show!" said Francine.

The next day, Max had another idea.

"Hey, Francine, want to play school?"

"Sure," said Francine. "I'll be the teacher."

"Okay," said Max. "You can be the teacher...and I'll be the principal."